A White Deer
And Other Stories

PATRICK D. SMITH

Other Works by Patrick D. Smith

Novels
THE RIVER IS HOME

THE BEGINNING

FOREVER ISLAND

ANGEL CITY

ALLAPATTAH

A LAND REMEMBERED

THE SEAS THAT MOURN

Non-Fiction
THE LAST RIDE (Co-Author)

IN SEARCH OF THE RUSSIAN BEAR

DVD
PATRICK SMITH'S FLORIDA,
A SENSE OF PLACE

ISBN 978-0-9765509-9-0
Library of Congress Control Number: 2007907929

~ Introduction ~

These stories of my father's go back a long way. I read some of them when I was a child. He was much younger than I am now when he wrote them. I remember the cat he wrote about in *The Demise of Bester Boo Boo*. We lived in Oxford, Mississippi then. That story was real.

I was thrilled to learn that Dad had kept all of these stories safely tucked away in file folders. I was honored when he said I could publish them. When I read them as a young boy, in my wildest dreams I could not have imagined that one day I would publish them.

Re-reading these stories, I can see that even back when Dad was writing them, he was laying the foundation for his later literary work. The style is quintessential Patrick Smith. I'm sure he wrote them for the pure joy of writing; a writer has to write to hone his skills. He couldn't have known that one day he would author a beloved novel like *A Land Remembered*, write a book called *Forever Island* that would be printed in 46 countries, or have a novel like *Angel City* made into a movie. Back then he was working a day job in public relations, raising a family, and writing when he had the time and inspiration to do so. The honors and awards would come later.

It is my privilege to bring these stories out of the file folders where they have been patiently waiting and make them available for you to enjoy. Thanks, Dad.

Rick Smith (Patrick Smith, Jr.)

A White Deer And Other Stories by Patrick D. Smith
Copyright © 2007, by Patrick D. Smith

All rights reserved. No part of this book may be reproduced in any form or by any means, electronic or mechanical, including photocopying, recording, or by an information storage and retrieval system, without permission in writing from the publisher.

Inquiries should be addressed to:

Panorama Studios
P.O. Box 343
Cambria, CA 93428

www.AWhiteDeer.com
www.PanoramaStudios.com

Library of Congress Control Number: 2007907929

Smith, Patrick D., 1927-
    A White Deer And Other Stories by Patrick D. Smith
ISBN 978-0-9765509-9-0

Printed in the United States of America

In This Volume

A White Deer

Journey Into Karma

Miss Jenny And The Minnows

The Demise Of Bester Boo Boo

A Pair Of Blue Shoes

Fried Mullet And Grits

Talk To The Wind - A Poem

A White Deer

A WHITE DEER

His bare feet splattered little puffs of dust as Dave Warren walked along the dirt road leading to the store. The sun was high in the sky and drew beads of sweat from Dave's chestnut-colored body, which was bare from the waist up. Occasionally he stopped and threw a clod of dirt into the bayou and watched with interest as the round ripples spread away from the splash. The long rows of the cotton fields stretched away toward the woods; the air of spring was filled with the sweet, tangy smell of freshly turned earth.

"Sure wish we could git a good rain afore long," Dave muttered. He kicked at the ground with his feet. "Jest about as hard as a brick bat," he said.

As he strolled around the bend, the big, white-washed store of Jeff Willicot came into view. Several men were sitting on the porch, chewing tobacco and spitting into the dust. Willicot and Joe Turner were playing checkers, the home-made board resting between them on a small table. They glanced up when Dave started up the steps.

"Howdy, Dave," Mr. Willicot said as he jumped one of Joe Turner's kings. "Go on in. Lucy's inside."

Dave's heart skipped a beat at the mention of Lucy. When he opened the screen door and walked inside, the contrast of the bright sunlight on the outside and the dimness of the inside caused him to blink his eyes.

The old store was crammed to the point of bursting with merchandise, and smelled heavily of leather and tobacco and hoop cheese. Saddles, harnesses, well buckets, wash tubs, plow points, and stocks, logging chains, canned goods, liniment—a thousand things all piled upon each other and filling shelves along the walls made a tangled jungle of the dim interior of the country store. Willicot's was the only store for ten miles, so he had to stock everything a Delta farmer might need.

Lucy Willicot was sitting behind a counter, shooing flies from a barrel of soda crackers. Lucy was the same age as Dave, going on sixteen. Dave and Lucy had gone to school together until the fifth grade; then Dave's father died and Dave quit school to run the small farm with his mother. To Dave, Lucy was the prettiest girl in all of the Steel Bayou country.

Dave walked up to the counter and looked directly at Lucy, then he shifted his gaze downward to his bare feet. He put his hands behind him and shuffled his feet one behind the other.

"Hello, Dave," Lucy said.

"Howdy, Miss Lucy," Dave replied, still shuffling. "Them flies givin' you trouble?" he asked.

"Flies always give us trouble in the spring. How's the plowing coming along?"

"Not too good. Looks like it's gonna be a mite slow if'n we don't get rain afore long. Ground's a might hard."

"Papa says we're going to get rain in a few days," Lucy said, putting down the fly swatter. "You want something, Dave?" she asked.

"I want a number ten plow point charged to us."

Lucy took the plow point from a rack and handed it to Dave. He looked at her hesitantly, as if he had something more to say, then he turned to leave.

"I hope you get rain before long," Lucy said.

"Thanks, Miss Lucy," he replied as he walked out the door.

Joe Turner had lost the checker game and now Biff Lumkin was playing with Mr. Willicot. Dave wanted to get in the game, but they had never asked him to play.

As Dave started down the steps, Emil Shorter spat a stream of brown tobacco juice across Dave's feet. Dave looked down at his feet, then he looked at Emil Shorter, a mixture of anger and humiliation glaring from his eyes.

"Seed that big white buck lately?" Emil Shorter asked, laughing. "You ain't been seein' white buzzards too, has you?"

All the men on the porch looked at Dave and laughed. Dave wanted to jump onto the porch and fight them all, but his mother had cautioned him to never fight except to defend himself, so he remembered this and hesitated.

"Why don't you grow up, boy?" Emil Shorter said, still laughing. "Goin' 'round claimin' you seen a white buck! Everbody in these parts knows they ain't no white buck in the Mississippi Delta. Maybe they's such a critter up in Canada or New England or sommers up there, but not here. If they were one here, I'd a seen him."

Mr. Willicot looked up from the checker game. "Why don't you fellows leave Dave be?" he said.

"That tale he tells 'bout a white buck ain't no more a whopper than some of the tales you fellows tell. And besides, Dave might have seen one; you don't know. Now go on 'bout your business, Dave," he said, going back to the checker game.

Dave tried to wipe the tobacco juice from his feet on the bottom porch step, but only smeared it. He turned and hurried down the road, wanting to get away as fast as he could from the sound of laughter. He hoped Lucy hadn't seen Emil Shorter spit on his feet. He broke into a trot and rounded the bend, then he came back along the bayou. When he came to a path that led down to the water he scrambled down the bank to wash the tobacco juice from his feet.

The cool water felt good to Dave; he stooped down and splashed some on his face. He heard a thumping on the path behind him and looked up. Old Uncle Jeffro, the aged black man who lived alone in a cabin in the big woods, was coming down the path, a cane pole in one hand, a can of worms in the other. People all over the Steel Bayou country knew Uncle Jeffro, and speculated on his age; but nobody knew how old he really was or where he had come from. Everyone admitted, however, that Uncle Jeffro knew every inch of the Steel Bayou better than any other man alive.

"Howdy, Mr. Dave," the old black man said. "How come you ain't in the fields, bustin' up the ground?"

"Broke a plow point, Uncle Jeffro," Dave said. "Jest comin' back from the store with a new one."

Uncle Jeffro sat down and started unwinding the line from around the cane pole. "Thought I'd see if'n them catfish done got hongry today," he said.

"Uncle Jeffro," Dave said, "do you believe they's such a thing as a white deer around these parts?"

Uncle Jeffro glanced at Dave with a surprised look. "Why they sho' do be such a thing, Mr. Dave," he said. "You the fust person ever axed me 'bout that white buck. I sees him some, an I 'member his ole pappy what used to gallivant about at night, scarin' the livin' fire outen folks an makin' 'um think he were a ghost. That were back afore most folks around here now can 'member."

"I've seed that deer three time," Dave said. "One day he come by the lower end of my field, and I thought I were just seein' things. Then I seed him twice after that in the woods, and I knowed he were real. But I ain't never seed him close enough to git a shot at him. I got to kill that white buck, Uncle Jeffro."

"You got a mighty big job on yo' hands, Mr. Dave," Uncle Jeffro said. "That buck's 'bout the smartest deer ever lived in these parts. You the fust one I ever heard done even seed him. What you want to kill him fer, Mr. Dave? He be's too purdy to kill. He's God's chile, an it would be like killin' Jesus."

"That buck hide mean a mighty heap to me," Dave said. "I need to take the hide to the store."

The old black man strung a worm on his hook and cast it into the edge of the water, close to a log, and stuck the pole into the bank. Then he settled back again. "Mistuh Dave," he said, "you know where that field of wild rye grass is, way up in the north end of Yonkipen Flats, close in on the swamp?"

"I been there a few times."

"Well, that white buck's feedin' there. I seed him last night. They's a trail at the south end that goes back into the swamp, an he starts back on that trail 'bout dawn. Only way I figger you can git that deer is to lay up on the trail an waylay him on his way back to the swamp. But, mistuh Dave, be mighty careful. They's bear an wild hog in them woods an swamps."

"I be careful," Dave said. "I sure thank you for tellin' me all this. I'm gone get that buck afore long."

"One more thing," Uncle Jeffro said. "If you get close, look to the eyes. If that buck has pink eyes, he be's a albino, a sort of a freak. If he has brown or gray eyes, he be's a natural born white deer. But no matter the eyes, remember he's God's chile."

Dave said again, "Thanks, Uncle Jeffro," then he climbed back up the bank. The sun was now beating down with the full heat of the day and it made him drowsy as he walked along kicking the dust. He would like to take a dip in the bayou, but he knew he must get home. His ma always wanted him to be on time for meals, and it was right at high noon.

Dave was glad to see the cypress head that covered the entrance to their clearing. He passed into the cool shade and walked along a trail that wound around the bases of giant trees. Green ferns and wild honeysuckle and dogwood bordered the trail. In a few minutes he came into the clearing and walked up to the side of the house.

Dave was proud of the house, although it was beginning to look as weathered as an old barn. When he was very young he had watched the cutting of the timber, watched as the frame went up and the boards were nailed into place, giving the house form. He was proud because he knew that his father had built it—built it with sweat and pride, and it belonged to them. Someday he would paint it, and then it would look new again. He walked around to the kitchen entrance and climbed the steps.

His ma was just putting the boiled collards, corn pone and salt pork on the table. "Get the plow point?" she asked.

"Yessum," Dave replied. "I laid it on the back steps."

They sat at the table and Dave's ma gave thanks before they started eating. Ma was not an old woman, but the strain of her hard life made her appear much older than her years. She had helped clear the land after they had purchased their forty acres, and she had helped cut the trees and saw them into lumber for the house. She also went into the fields and worked beside her husband as they planted the cotton seed and picked the fluffy fibers in late summer and fall. But she never complained. She worked day after day with no thought of someday never having to work again.

"Ma," Dave said, "if' n you don't mind, I ain't goin' to do no more plowin' till we get some rain and the ground is soft. Couldn't plant seed nohow till we get some rain."

"That suits me fine," she said. "We got time yet to get the crop in the ground. What you plannin' on doin' till it rain?"

"I'm goin' after that white buck deer I been tellin' you 'bout. I run into Uncle Jeffro an he told me where that deer is layin' up an eatin' at night."

"They teased you up to the store 'bout that deer again?" she asked. "They done made you mad, ain't they?"

"They ain't said too much," Dave said. "I just wants to kill that deer."

"I know how you feels, son," Ma said. "Ever' man looks for a white deer, but some never finds him. This farm was your pa's white deer but he killed hisself workin' it. If you go after that deer, be careful. An if'n you git him, an he don't do what you wants him to do, don't fret none. If'n you don't git him, don't fret neither."

"I'll git him," Dave said, a determined note in his voice.

As soon as the meal was finished Dave took his hunting knife and rifle and set out toward Yonkipen Flats. He crossed his own field and figured in his mind how long it would take to finish the plowing that he had not already done. If the crop came out good this year, he might even be able to paint the house.

When he left the field, the country took on a different look. He was on the outer edge of the great Yonkipen Swamp. Water oak and cypress and hickory and sweet gum trees stood silently reaching for the sky. Buck vines and thorn bushes blocked every opening; he often had to crawl for long stretches to make any progress. He marked a trail with his hunting knife so that he would be able to follow the same trail later. After more than an hour the vines thinned out some, and he came to the small clearing Uncle Jeffro had told him about.

Dave walked around the clearing and examined the wild rye grass. He could see that the deer had been grazing there. Deer droppings were scattered about in small clumps. He continued searching until he found the trail the deer were using to go back into the swamp. He walked down the trail for a short distance, seeing where buck antlers had snagged the vines and skinned bark from trees.

He finally found a place where the trail widened, a perfect spot to lie in ambush for the white buck. He marked the spot with his knife and started back home.

All during the return trip Dave thought about how he would go after the deer. It would be no use to shoot at night because if he merely wounded it, he could never follow it through the darkness of the swamp. He would have to go to his ambush spot that evening, stay all night, and try to get the deer when it left the clearing at dawn. The wind would have to be right, else the buck would smell him and avoid the trail. Dave was so occupied with his thoughts that the sun had reddened the western sky and he was back at the field before he realized it. He hurried across the clearing toward the barn to do his evening chores.

After supper Dave sat on the back steps and watched the moon creep slowly above the tree tops, bathing the clearing with silver light. He somehow felt as if he was just starting on the greatest thing he had ever done in his life. He was not afraid, although a tingle of doubt mixed with excitement raced through his body. He knew that if he was careful he would be in no great danger, and he knew it was possible that his first shot would kill the buck on the spot and it would all be over. He thought about Lucy, wondering what she would think when he had painted the house a glowing white. He looked at the moon a long time, listening to the night call of the birds.

Ma came to the back steps and looked at him in silence, then she said, "I got you a sweet tater and some corn pone case you gits hungry afore you make it back."

Dave got up and checked the old Winchester to see that it was fully loaded, then he strapped the hunting knife to his side. Ma handed him the sack of food.

"You be real careful, son," she said as she leaned over and kissed him on the cheek.

"I will, Ma," he said. "Don't you worry none."

When Dave started across the yard, his hunting dog, Rink, howled in anticipation, pulling against the leash which held him to a fence post. Dave patted the dog on the head but did not release him. He could not chance the howl Rink would surely make if he smelled deer. Absolute silence would be a necessity.

Ma stood on the steps and watched Dave as he crossed the back yard, watched as he walked down the path towards the field and was swallowed up by the night. Somewhere far away, the shrill cry of a screech owl shattered the silence. Ma looked fondly after the boy long after he disappeared, then she finally turned and walked back into the house.

Dave crossed the field and hesitated for a few minutes before plunging into the woods. The moonlight was so bright he could see every detail of the field and the bordering woods. He was glad, for it would make traveling in the woods easier. He glanced back at the house, seeing the dim glow of a kerosene lamp spilling softly from a window, then he entered the woods where he had marked the first tree that afternoon.

The freshly cut scars on vines and trees were visible in the moonlight, making it easy for him to follow the trail he had blazed for himself. When he crawled under thick mattings of vines a tingle of fear raced through him, knowing that rattlesnakes were out this time of year. He could hear sounds of the animal and bird kingdoms that come to life at night, but no warning rattles. He followed the trail slowly and cautiously until the clearing lay but a short distance ahead.

He skirted the south end of the clearing but did not try to get close enough to see if the deer were there, not wanting to take any chance they would sense his presence. He inched along until he came to the trail leading to the swamp, then he left the trail and crept along until he found the lie-up place he had marked that afternoon. He quietly scraped the ground clear of leaves and twigs so that if he had to move around, he could do so without noise. Then he sat on the ground and surveyed the world around him.

The moon was now high overhead, and the giant cypress trees were silhouetted one against the other. A slight breeze, blowing from the north, rustled the tree limbs. Dave lay on his back and looked upward at the star-speckled sky. It was a strange feeling, being alone in the woods at night so far from home, isolated from all that was familiar. He had planned to stay awake all night watching the trail, but he was tired, more tired than he realized, and very soon sleep pressed upon him so gently he did not know when it came.

Dave awoke with a start, seeing that the first streaks of dawn were piercing the eastern sky. He thought he heard a gentle thumping on the trail, and then it came again. He eased the rifle from the ground and flicked the safety, then he sat in dead silence, afraid to let even his breath make a sound. He heard the thumping move toward him and stop, then move forward again. Looking up the trail, he saw a vine move. He raised the rifle and pointed it in the direction of the movement. He gripped the stock tightly to steady his shaking hands. Just then a small doe bounded along the trail and passed without seeing him. Dave's heart made a huge lump in his throat.

In his excitement, he had not noticed the wind. It was blowing directly into his face, placing him downwind of the trail where the deer would not smell him. This encouraged him, but he was angry with himself for almost pulling the trigger when the doe came by, which would have ruined everything.

Three more does bounded down the trail and passed without seeing him. Dave knew the bucks always sent the does out ahead of them, that the bucks would soon follow. He fought against the trembling in his hands. Three more does came down the trail, then silence fell again.

Dave listened intently and could hear a slight tinkling.

He knew the sound—a buck was coming down the trail, its antlers striking the vines. He raised the rifle again and waited. The buck trotted into the small clearing and passed. It was a beautiful buck. Dave counted fourteen points on the antlers, but its hide was brown. This buck was followed by several more, some young and some old, but all with brown hides. Then they stopped coming. Dave felt a chill surge through his veins. He wondered if the white buck had passed while he was asleep, or if the buck had not gone out that night; then he wondered if the white buck actually existed, or if it was just a dream. His spirits sank as he sat watching the empty trail.

He sat for what seemed like hours but was no more than ten minutes. Nothing came down the trail. Squirrels chattered in the trees above him. High above, crows cawed as they moved about in search of food.

He was just about to give up when he heard a slight rustle to his left. He turned slowly, then his hands froze to the rifle. Only twenty yards distant, silhouetted against the thick vines, stood the biggest buck he had ever seen, a great white patch against the brown of the vines.

Dave threw up the rifle and the buck disappeared behind the vines. Tears welled in his eyes, and he was furious with himself because he had not guessed that the white buck would be too smart to use the trail, that it would go along parallel to the trail. He heard another noise behind the vines, then the buck jumped into view again. Dave aimed, but his finger froze to the trigger as he heard the words, "…God's chile ... like killin' Jesus…" The buck hesitated for only a moment, then it leaped past the vines and disappeared.

As soon as the deer disappeared, Dave thought about the eyes. He had not looked into the buck's eyes. He did not know if they were brown or pink, and now this mattered a great deal to him. He would follow the deer until they were face to face with each other. He immediately started tracking the buck.

The ground under Dave's feet soon became soft, and he knew he was heading directly into the swamp. He had hoped the deer would veer along the edge of the swamp, but this was not to be. Several times he heard the buck ahead of him, but traveling as fast as he could, he had not seen it again.

Giant green ferns now blocked Dave's trail, and rotted limbs and decayed leaves gave way beneath his feet. If it had not been for the dry spell, he would be sinking up to his knees in muck, and could not possibly follow the deer. The sunlight, turned away by thick trees, was merely a twilight haze, giving the swamp an eerie, unearthly atmosphere. Occasionally Dave had to wade through pools of green slime, and cottonmouth moccasins slithered away from his path. Fear enveloped him constantly, and he prayed silently that the brown death would not strike as he invaded this strange world not intended for man.

When he finally stopped to rest, he realized it was well past noon, and he had not eaten or taken a drink of water since the previous night. He knew that drinking swamp water was out of the question, but he took a piece of corn pone and the baked sweet potato from his sack and ate greedily. He dared not eat the salt pork for fear of the thirst becoming worse. After he had rested a few moments, he continued his relentless pursuit.

The tracks of the buck in the soft earth were easy to follow. Dave studied the position of the sun and realized the buck was now gradually turning north, away from the swamp. Dave thought he knew approximately where he was, and figured that the buck was heading toward Chotard Lake.

He doggedly followed the trail and gradually came back onto firmer ground. The sun was low in the sky when he stopped to rest again. He had followed the trail all day and hadn't seen the buck since early that morning.

Night was now coming on, and this made Dave push on faster. As long as he headed north, he knew he would eventually come back to Steel Bayou. He hoped the deer would not suddenly turn in a different direction. He kept following the tracks, and just as the sun was sinking, he broke through a thick clump of willows and stood on the bank of the bayou. He saw where the deer tracks had sunk into the soft mud; then, looking across the water, he saw the tracks go up the other side.

Dave fell to his knees and pushed his face under the cool water. He bathed the cuts that covered his face and arms, cuts he had not noticed until now. Then he slipped into the water and swam to the other side, holding the gun and food sack above his head. After he climbed the opposite bank he ate the remainder of the food and then lay on the ground, deciding not to follow the trail until morning. He put his hands over his eyes and realized he was tired, very tired. The cuts on his body were stinging, and his leg muscles ached with pain. In a few moments he fell into a restless sleep.

Dave awoke before dawn and could not see the stars. The wind was thrashing the tree limbs against each other, and he did not like the sound of the wind. Far in the distance, white fingers of lightening cut through the darkness. When he stood up he discovered he was stiff and sore, so he sat back down and waited patiently for the dawn, which was long in coming.

When light finally broke through, it was eerie and grayish-yellow, the color of molasses. Rumbling black clouds boiled over the tree tops. Dead limbs broke from trees and splashed into the bayou. The wind turned cooler, making Dave shiver in his thin cotton shirt. A storm was blowing in, and he knew he should turn for home; but he also knew he would never give up the trail until he had seen the deer again. He turned and started following the tracks.

He had walked but a short distance when he heard the buck ahead of him, and he realized they had spent the night no more than fifty yards apart. His heart pounded madly, for he knew it was now possible that he would see the deer again, that the long chase would come to an end. He walked slowly at first, then he rushed blindly through everything that stood in his way. His eyes flashed with unbelieving surprise when he felt a hot, searing pain shoot up his right leg and saw his own red blood spurt out ahead of him. He felt himself being lifted into the air and rolled backward. For a moment he was stunned senseless, but he sat up quickly.

Dave felt only astonishment as he watched the wild boar turn in a half circle and stop, facing him, blood dripping from its tusks. He had not seen it when he ran up on it, and didn't know what had hit him. The boar grunted and pawed the ground, ready to charge again. Dave knew he was facing the most dangerous foe of the woods, that the boar could rip the insides out of him with one swipe. He could not understand why this impartial obstacle had been placed in his path just when success seemed so near. The boar hesitated before charging, studying the thing that faced him. The frenzied animal seemed to be as perplexed as the frightened boy it intended to kill. Suddenly a blinding sheet of rain pounded down upon them.

A white sheet suddenly rushed from a clump of vines, and the antlers smashed into the boar's side, causing it to squeal with both surprise and pain as it rolled over the ground rapidly. As it tried to get up, the antlers caught it again; then it struggled up and ran away.

Dave stared with disbelief as the white buck looked at him momentarily with huge brown eyes. From behind the vines there suddenly appeared a white doe and a white fawn, both with brown eyes. They looked at the boy for a split second, then all three of them turned and disappeared rapidly into the woods. Dave then knew why the buck had attacked the wild boar. It was to protect the fawn.

Dave knew he must get back across the bayou before the rain swelled it, then he should head up the bayou until he found familiar ground, and make his way home from there. He must get home before dark, for he was too weak to survive another night in the woods. He cut a sleeve from his shirt and bound the wound, trying to stop the flow of blood, then he limped away toward the bayou.

The pounding rain had turned the bank of the bayou into muddy slush. When he started down his feet slipped, and Dave rolled into the edge of the water. He lay still for a few moments, letting the swirling water rush over his body, then he pushed himself away from the bank. No thought of danger entered his mind. The current caught him and rushed him downstream, and finally he felt his feet touch the soft mud of the opposite bank.

He had no idea of time or space or how long he had been in the water. The bayou was rising rapidly, and the current pushed hard against him. He slowly pulled himself up the bank, then he started walking blindly again.

His torn leg was numb now, and he felt no pain as he stumbled across logs and pushed through vines. The storm moved in with its full fury, lashing trees against each other. The angry boom of thunder seemed to make the ground tremble, and fingers of white split tree limbs, showering the ground with wood chips.

When Dave could move no further he fell to his back in the mud. He lay still with his eyes closed, and visions flashed through his mind. He could see a gleaming white house. On the porch, dressed in a freshly starched apron, sat Lucy. His mother was inside, cooking yard eggs and corn pone and salt pork. Long rows of cotton burst forth into a billowing sea of fluffy fiber. He saw a giant checker board covered with human forms, laughing and spitting tobacco juice. Then he saw a majestic white buck, standing proudly erect in the forest. You be mighty careful, Mistuh Dave. Then darkness rushed in and blocked all thought from his mind.

When Dave finally looked up, rain was pounding into his face and he could hardly see; but slowly and dimly, the shape of a giant cypress tree broke into his vision. He sat up quickly, wiped the water from his eyes, and looked again. The tree had a fork in its top. He knew the tree, and he knew where he was. Many times he had seen the giant forked tree from the cow pasture, and he often wished he could climb it. Hope now fired him, and he slowly struggled to his feet.

From where he stood the bayou made a sweeping curve to the north and came back close to his house. Following the bayou, it was three miles to their clearing; but if he cut straight across the flats, it was only a half-mile to the cow pasture. Most of the year the flats were a bog and impossible to cross, but maybe the rain had not yet softened them too much. He decided he would take the chance.

He stood at the base of the giant tree and sighted in the direction of the cow pasture, then he stumbled forward. At first the ground was not soft, but it gradually turned into muck, sinking him above the ankles and sucking his shoes. The going became slower and slower until finally he sank down to his knees. He had to pull one leg out and place it ahead of him before he pulled the other out, and this caused intense pain.

He finally realized he could not go on this way, yet he knew he was more than halfway across the flats. The rain had stopped soaking into the ground and had formed a lake, and he could see no ground at all. He pulled himself forward until he had both legs out of the muck and was lying on his stomach, then he started slowly crawling forward until his head was almost under water.

His senses dulled again, but he continued moving by instinct. He stopped when he felt his head hit something solid. The jar brought him back to his senses again, and he looked up. Above him he could see strands of barbed wire, see that he had bumped into one of the pasture fence posts; and dimly, through the sheets of rain, he could see the outline of the house. There was almost no light at all, but he had made it. He crawled under the fence and pulled himself to his feet.

He staggered weakly, then he broke into a trot. He ran to the rear of the house and climbed the kitchen steps, then he pushed open the door and tumbled inside. Before another sea of darkness swept over him he could see the surprised look on his mother's face as she cried, "Dave! Dave! You're home!"

When Dave awoke, the sun was streaming through the window and onto his bed. He glanced around and saw his mother in the doorway, looking at him. He swung out from under the quilt, put his feet on the floor and said, "How long I been in bed, Ma?"

"Two days. You ain't even woke up to take your meals. You done give me the worst scare I ever had, son."

"Didn't mean to, Ma. But I had a good scare myself, especially with that wild boar. He might have done me in except for that white buck."

"I've been taking care of that gash on your leg. It may be sore for awhile, but it's O.K. And I hope you won't go chasin' that deer again."

"I won't, Ma," Dave said. "You can count on that. Now how about some vittles. I could eat a skunk."

"Don't serve that," Ma chuckled, "but I'll fix up something soon as you get dressed. And I know you want to go to the store and see Lucy."

Dave blushed, and then he said, "Aw, Ma, how come you to say that?"

"A mother knows," she smiled.

Ma stood on the front porch and watched him as he started through the cypress head. She noticed something was different about his stride, something about him had changed since that day he walked alone into the woods seeking the white deer, carrying with him a determination to kill it. She smiled as he passed from her sight.

Before he realized it, he had come around the bend and the store came into view. As usual, the men were sitting on the porch, waiting their turns at the checker board, chewing tobacco and spitting into the road. They did not see him coming.

Dave came around the side of the store and was halfway up the steps before they noticed him.

He walked over to Mr. Willicot and said, "I need some bandage tape, Mr. Willicot. I cut my leg the other day."

"Go on in," Willicot responded. "Lucy's inside. She'll get it for you."

Joe Turner turned to Dave and said, "Seen that white deer again?"

Dave did not dare tell them about the doe and the fawn or they would tease him forever. He said, "Yes, I seen him, and he is gone"

"Gone?" Turner questioned. "Gone where?"

"He was headed north, so I suppose he's gone to the Tennessee mountains, back where he probably came from. I don't expect to ever see him again." With that he turned and went into the store.

Lucy was standing behind the counter, and Dave walked up to her and said, "I need some tape, Miss Lucy. I cut my leg and Ma is out of tape."

She went to a shelf, came back and handed him the tape, then she said, "Don't call me Miss Lucy anymore, Dave. Just call me Lucy."

Dave's heart skipped a beat as she smiled at him. He turned to leave and fell over the cracker barrel. He jumped to his feet and backed out the door.

When he started down the steps, Mr. Willicot said, "Just a minute, Dave boy. Joe and Emil and all the others say it's your turn at the checkers, if'n you got time for a game."

"I ain't got the time," Dave responded quickly, keeping the surprise to himself. "I've got too much work to do."

"Maybe the next time," Mr. Willicot said. "You'll always be welcome."

"Thanks," Dave said as he walked away.

Journey Into Karma

JOURNEY INTO KARMA

James Drury Allen sat of the edge of a bed in the motel room, watching his wife toy with her hair in front of the mirror. She's still a good looking woman even at forty-two, he thought, having an urge to tell her how much he appreciated her not having allowed herself to deteriorate after enduring twenty-two years of marriage and the birth and rearing of two children. The blonde hair showed few traces of gray, and the green eyes still had the sparkle of youth. He shifted his thoughts away from her when he remembered his reason for being in San Diego.

He got up, took his coat from the closet and put it on, then he walked to the door and hesitated, wondering if he were doing the right thing, thinking that perhaps they should leave this place immediately and let sleeping phantoms lie, that perhaps it was an error even to have returned. But he knew he would take this walk regardless. This was what he had come for, his reason for being here. San Diego was where it had happened. *Or had it?* For a moment he was not sure. Sometimes the whole thing seemed unreal, imaginary. *Twenty-four years. Impossible!* he thought. Or was it? Was it twenty-four hours or twenty-four years or twenty-four thousand years or not at all? he asked himself. But it was real. He knew. He needed no visible physical scar to prove it to himself. The scar that had bothered him all these years was one no one else could see, no one but himself knew to exist—a scar on his soul, self-inflicted, the kind that festers and grows larger, never to heal.

He must walk these streets again, *to prove what?*—nothing really, he thought, but this was a path he must retrace and wanted to retrace, here where it had happened. Then he thought again, *Or had it?*

"I'm going for a walk, Cathy," he said, opening the door and letting the bright mid-winter California sunshine spill into the room. "I won't be gone long."

She looked at him for a moment in silence, then she said, "Take your time, Jimmy. I'm going to take a nap. I'm still kinda tired from the trip." She knew they had not come here all the way from Burley, Kentucky merely on a mid-winter vacation. Not to San Diego. He had come to prove something to himself. Whatever it was, she would not interfere. If he had a dragon to kill, he must slay it alone.

He closed the door gently and stood for a moment looking at the palm trees and blue sky, the traffic moving slowly along the street. Then he began to walk, seemingly aimless but with purpose, moving nonchalantly toward a specific destination. He appeared to be no different from any other tourist who could afford a mid-winter vacation in California. And he could afford this trip. He was the senior partner in the law firm of Allen, Touart and Billings. He owned a brick four-bedroom house, two cars and a fishing boat; he had an American Express card and a Diners Club card; he had served as president of both the local Rotary Club and the Chamber of Commerce. They belonged to the country club. His son was a senior at the State University and his daughter a freshman. Judged by most current standards, James Drury Allen was a successful man. Not wealthy, but comfortably successful. But he was also a man haunted by an invisible phantom.

Nothing looked familiar—not as he remembered it. It seemed as if he were in this city for the first time. Everything was strange until he came to the park, the small park with palm trees and green benches, then it all rushed back to him. He found the exact bench, the exact spot where it had happened that night twenty-four years ago. He was sure, for this one small space was etched into his memory.

Suddenly he could see the eyes, the tired brown eyes not filled with accusation or hostility or fear, but with sympathy; then he could hear the voice, gentle and kind, *You didn't have to do that, son. If you'd asked, I'd have given it to you.*

The mission house was just across the street. At least, that's where it was then. Maybe now it is a pawn shop or a restaurant or a parking lot, he thought. He started to walk away in that direction, then he hesitated, turned back and sat on the bench. He stared blankly out across the park and drifted backward through time, remembering ...

Jimmy Allen was nineteen when he dropped out of college in 1942 and joined the navy. He was sent to San Diego for boot training. The city had the atmosphere of a carnival mixed with apprehension and fear. Thousands of frightened young boys were desperately trying to hide the fear by grasping at anything they considered at the time to be a distraction from the reality of war and what they faced in the future. The atmosphere was one of faked expressions of unconcern expressed in bars, senseless fights among themselves, honky-tonk love which meant nothing, and wild abandon: one last fling before being sent out to war, perhaps never to return. Whatever they had been before arriving in San Diego, or whatever they might someday be, was temporarily forgotten.

Jimmy Allen's time came immediately after boot training ended. He was assigned to a destroyer, and three days later the expected news swept over the ship: they would leave tomorrow. The last night ashore. Most of the boys would make the best of it, regardless.

But not Jimmy Allen, one of the rare exceptions. He stayed on board after most of his shipmates had departed. Not all of them would make a reckless frolic of this last night ashore, but most would. Some would seek a chapel. Jimmy Allen wrote letters—some he knew he should write, and some to people who would not expect to hear from him. Putting words on paper seemed to take some of the tension from him. Then he left the ship and walked aimlessly, going nowhere in particular, just drifting. And then he went into the bar, a small tavern where he met Tony Marcellus from Chicago.

They drank beer and talked. Tony was peculiar—different somehow. Jimmy had never known anyone like him. When he asked Tony why he had enlisted, Tony said, "Well, why not? Back in Chicago when you shoot at somebody the cops get after you. Here they train you how to shoot, and you get paid for doing it. Doesn't matter to me if I'm shooting at a street punk or a Jap. It's all the same to me." Then he gulped down the last of his beer and said, "I'm broke, Jim-Bo. You got any dough?"

"I don't even have taxi fare left," Jimmy said, watching Tony's slender fingers nervously grasp the empty glass. "It'll be a long walk back to the base." Jimmy started to get up, then he said absently, "Guess I won't need any money for awhile anyway, not after tonight. My ship leaves tomorrow."

"Christ!" Tony said sharply, ignoring Jimmy momentarily. My tub is supposed to leave tomorrow too, and I'm not near done with shore leave." Then he looked up and said, "Come on, Jim-Bo. We'll get some loot."

"How? Jimmy asked, puzzled.

"We'll roll somebody," Tony said casually. "You think I went to school on the streets of Chicago for nothing? Come on, I'll show you."

Jimmy could not tell if Tony was serious or joking. He followed him from the bar reluctantly. They walked silently for two blocks, then they turned a corner and stopped across the street from a dimly-lit building. There was a faded red sign above the entrance: SAN JOSE MISSION. It was one of those places where you could get a bowl of soup for a dime, and if you didn't have a dime, it was free; and there were cots priced at fifty-cents per night, and if you didn't have a half-dollar, it was free. The second floor contained rooms which were rented to permanent residents for thirty dollars a month.

They watched silently as a man came from the building and stood idly in the yellow glow of a street lamp. To them he seemed ancient but was probably no more than fifty. His clothes were outdated and worn, shabby but cared for. He did not look like a bum to Jimmy. He seemed to have the same humble dignity of a hundred farmers Jimmy had seen dressed the same way. Perhaps he was just temporarily down on his luck, or had been struck by some tragedy in his life, and was yet to recover.

Tony studied the man for a moment, and then he said, "You see that old coot, Jim-Bo. That's the kind will fool you. They'll live in them flophouses so's they can save every dime they get their hands on. One lived close to me in Chicago. When he died, the cops found over a thousand dollars stuffed in his mattress. That one over yonder is probably a miser, too. Come on."

Jimmy felt a strong urge to run, to turn back and leave Tony Marcellus, but again he followed him reluctantly—mostly, he felt, out of a sense of curiosity. In a strange way, Tony Marcellus fascinated him. They crossed the street and approached the old man. Tony said, "How about having a drink with us, Pop?"

The man's face flashed surprise, then pleasure. He was obviously flattered. He said quickly, "It'll be my pleasure." And then he said expectantly,

"The treat's on me, if you'll take a glass of beer."

"Sure, Pop, beer's fine," Tony said.

They walked together along the street, the old man in the middle, chattering constantly. He said, "I had a son, and if it hadn't happened, he'd be about your age. That was a long time ago, back when we had our own place in the country." He stopped for a moment, then he said, "He'd a sure joined up with you fellows to fight the war. He'd a had on a uniform too ... if it hadn't happened. His mamma would have been real proud of him. Sammy was—"

Jimmy said, "What happ—?"

"Let's cut across the park," Tony interrupted quickly. "There's a beer joint just over there."

Each time Jimmy tried to find out something about the old man's life, Tony would break in with some insignificant remark, anything to stop the conversation and keep them as strangers. When they reached a deserted spot in the park Tony stopped and said, "Pop, how long you been livin' in that flophouse?"

The answer never came out. Tony smashed his fist into the old man's stomach, causing him to double up in pain; then he hit him in the face, knocking him to the ground. Tony leaned down and snatched out the wallet, then he said sharply, "It's empty!" He threw the wallet aside, searched the man's pockets and said, "Two dollars and forty cents. Hell, it wadn't worth it. We'll have to find us another one. Let's go, Jim-Bo, before the old flea-bag gets his breath back and yells for the cops."

Jimmy stood frozen, paralyzed, not wanting to believe what he had seen, yet realizing he was a part of it merely by his presence. He had gone along with Tony, but he didn't really believe Tony would do it. Jimmy tried to speak, but couldn't. Then Tony said urgently, "Let's move! You want your tail thrown in the can?"

Jimmy still didn't move as Tony turned and ran from the park. The old man pushed himself up and looked at Jimmy, his eyes not reflecting accusation or hostility or fear, but sympathy. Jimmy waited for the man to scream or curse or shout for help, but he did not do so. He locked his eyes directly into Jimmy's eyes and said softly, "You didn't have to do that, son. If you'd asked, I'd have given it to you."

Jimmy said falteringly, "I'm…" But he never finished. He couldn't look further into the eyes, eyes that were burning a brand into his memory. He turned and ran in the opposite direction from Tony Marcellus, leaving the old man still lying on the ground.

Jimmy never saw Tony Marcellus again or San Diego again, but he saw the eyes. He saw them on every bulkhead, on every deck, inside every locker; he saw them on the tips of gunsights, on a hundred whitecaps, on a thousand stars. And he heard the voice, as if it were the voice of mankind, You didn't have to do that, son. *If you'd asked, I'd have given it to you.*

The war lasted only six months for Jimmy. His ship was bombed, and a piece of shrapnel passed through one of his lungs. He was sent home. He left the war behind, but he did not leave the eyes. Sometimes he would see them in a textbook, and sometimes he would see them in the eyes of a professor. Later, they appeared on the walls of his law office, in the faces of jurors. And sometimes he even saw them when he looked at Cathy. He wondered if somehow she could know; and then he would think: *Perhaps every woman knows that deep within her man there lies a phantom.* And the voice— sometimes the voice came from the mouths of his own children. He would also hear it on television, and from behind locked doors through which he could not see. As the years passed, he heard it less often, yet it was there, always there.

James Drury Allen got up from the bench and walked on through the park. He hoped the mission would still be there. If not, he would have to change his plans and do something else. He suddenly felt old and tired, very tired. His feet shuffled as he walked. He crossed the street and turned a corner. It was there, the same as he remembered it. A faded red sign came into view: SAN JOSE MISSION. A feeling of relief swept over him. He thought, Thank God. Now it can be done. It can end forever.

He took out his wallet and removed a bill. It was a thousand dollar bill, money he had saved from his first earnings as a lawyer. He had always intended to do this someday, and and now was the time. He crossed the street and entered the building.

People were sitting in worn chairs scattered around the lobby. He looked for the box. He knew that somewhere there would be a wooden box with a slit in the top into which contributions could be dropped. Soup couldn't be made either for a dime or for free. Someone had to pay. He found the box on the serving table. His hand trembled as he placed the bill into the slot and released it. Then he waited. He stood there silently, expecting a sudden brilliant flash of lightning to strike him, expecting a flood of release to rush from each of his pores. He wanted to be transformed, to be flushed free of the eyes and the voice, like the flushing of a toilet bowl. But he felt nothing. It was the same. The money had made no difference. A deep overwhelming sickness rushed through his body, melting his muscles. He felt defeated forever, hopeless. As he turned to leave, his face was contorted with disappointment, anguish and frustration. He looked as old and as lost as those about him.

And then he saw an old man sitting in a chair against the wall. He was as old as the man appeared to be to two young boys more than two decades ago. Something sprang into Jimmy and snapped him back to reality. He muttered aloud, "Could it be?...Could it?" And then he thought, *No, it's impossible. It's been too long. He was old then.* Yet he walked straight to the drowsing form and said, "How about having a drink with me, Pop?"

The old man looked up slowly. His eyes were brown and tired, but they showed no sign of recognition. As he stared at Jimmy his countenance of puzzlement changed almost imperceptibly to one of deep searching. Then for a moment, for just a fleeting second, a spark of remembrance flashed into his eyes. He smiled and said in a gentle voice, "It'll be my pleasure…" And then he said, "The treat's on me, if you'll take a glass of beer."

For a moment Jimmy's face turned ashen white. He swayed with an overwhelming feeling of faintness, then all the guilt and the sickness drained from his body and his mind in one tremendous rush. He said quickly, "Oh no, Pop, not on your life! This one's on me!"

He helped the old man from the chair and they left the building together.

Cathy awoke late in the afternoon and Jimmy had not returned. She showered and dressed, read a magazine, and then started to worry. She knew something was strange about this trip to San Diego, that Jimmy had not planned it merely as a vacation. They had never taken a mid-winter vacation. In fact, they had not gone away alone since the first child came. She wondered where he was and what he had been doing all day.

Cathy loved Jimmy very much, and they had enjoyed a good marriage. Yet always she had known that something troubled him, something deep inside that she could not see or share. She knew it in the way he sometimes became silent and preoccupied, gazing into something past her and the children, beyond their life together. She did not question this. If ever he wanted to speak, she would listen, but she would not pry. But now, for the first time, she was worried. This strange trip, she thought, this almost urgent desire to come to such an unlikely place on the pretense of a vacation. *Why?* She searched for an answer she knew she would not find.

Then came the knock. She opened the door anxiously and said as he entered, "Jimmy, where on earth have you been? I didn't expect you to be gone this long."

"Had a few beers with an old friend I met here a long time ago," he replied. Then he put his arms around her, smiled and said, "Cathy, have I told you how much I love you?"

"Yes, but it's always good to hear," she said, pleased but still puzzled. "But Jimmy…"

"You know what," he interrupted, pulling her closer to him, "I've decided it's time for a second honeymoon. Yessir, this trip is it. We'll start tonight by having the best dinner in San Diego, and champagne, then tomorrow we'll go to Acapulco, then to Mexico City, and on the way home we'll go by Miami, and—"

"Jimmy…Jimmy…slow down a second. I—"

"We'll have a wonderful time, honey," he said, his face beaming, "the most wonderful time of our lives." Then he looked deeply into Cathy's eyes, seeing her eyes only, and said again, "Cathy, have I ever told you how much I love you?"

Miss Jenny and the Minnows

MISS JENNY AND THE MINNOWS

"Clem, shudd-up! It's time for Miss Jenny to be here, and you know she'd faint dead-away if she heard you cussin' like that."

Clem Bailey looked up at the clock on the wall of Joe's Bait Shop. It was three minutes until two. He spat a bubbling stream of tobacco juice across the sidewalk, shifted the cud and said, "Sorry, Joe. I didn't think it was this near the time. I'll wait till after she's gone before I finish."

Joe Clayton said, "Well, you fellows be more careful. I don't mind you hanging around here every Friday afternoon to see Miss Jenny come in, but watch that cussin'. She'd have Preacher Hooker over to see me before sundown if she knew such trash is talked at my place. And I don't want no tiff with the preacher if it ain't necessary."

Marv Sutter looked up the street and squinted. He shifted his hat to the back of his head, straightened his body and said, "Here she comes, boys. She ain't gonna miss it by thirty seconds. Guess you'll win the pot this week, Buster." The line of men sitting on the two benches in front of the small store that sold bait and fishing tackle shifted positions, now sitting ramrod straight. Clem Bailey took the cud of tobacco from his mouth and held it in his hand.

Miss Jenny Lofton looked neither right nor left as she walked rapidly along the sidewalk, her high-topped shoes making a clicking sound against the concrete. A blue cotton dress swirled down to just above her ankles. She wore a wide-brimmed white hat covered with artificial flowers, and in her right hand she carried a quart Mason jar. She looked like something that had stepped from an illustrated page of a calendar dated fifty years in the past.

When she reached the bench-sitters, the men all tipped their hats solemnly and said in unison, "Afternoon, Miss Jenny." She nodded her head slightly without smiling, then she turned briskly into the store, leaving behind a strong odor of old cloth and chasteness.

Joe Clayton stood behind the counter, waiting. When she entered he said immediately, "Afternoon, Miss Jenny. Something I can do for you?" He knew without asking. Every Friday afternoon at almost the exact time for the past twenty years, Miss Jenny Lofton had come into his store and purchased the same thing.

She held the jar forward and said, as if saying it for the first time, "I would like one minnow, if you please."

Clayton took the jar and went back to the minnow vat. He filled the jar with water, picked up the net and trapped a large minnow. He always selected a healthy minnow for Miss Jenny. He dropped the minnow into the jar and returned to the counter. "That'll be two cents, Miss Jenny," he said formally, as if repeating lines he had memorized for a school play.

She carefully removed two copper coins from her purse and put them on the counter, then she picked up the jar and left quickly, without further conversation.

The men watched her retreat up the sidewalk, the long dress flapping behind her, the wide-brimmed hat bobbing like an umbrella in a high wind. One said, "What in tarnation you reckon she does with it?"

"I be damned if I know. She ain't never been fishing."

"Maybe she eats it. Some folks is plumb peculiar about what they'll put in their belly."

"Could be she's got a fish pool in her back yard and puts 'um there."

"T'aint so. Ole Biff Turner slipped over to her place one day while she was down here and searched the whole grounds. She ain't got no fish pool nowheres."

"What you reckon she does with it?"

"Don't know. Beats hell out of me."

Clem Bailey put the cud of tobacco back into his mouth, chewed, spat and said, ""Maybe she keeps 'urn in one of them goldfish bowls in the house."

"That ain't possible," another said quickly, "a minnow won't live without running water."

"I guess. But it pure beats hell out of me."

Miss Jenny continued her steady pace back along the street, wading unconcerned through the glances of those who were accustomed to seeing her trot along the sidewalk each Friday afternoon holding a quart Mason jar containing one minnow, and caring even less for those who were seeing and wondering for the first time. She moved as one with a predestined rendezvous, the tired pallid flesh of her face showing no sign of emotion, revealing no more of her inner self than as if she had been along the sidewalk carrying a loaf of bread instead of a Mason jar.

She left the business district and passed beneath the overhanging limbs of ancient oak trees, walked silently along three blocks of a residential area lined with weary two and three-story Victorian palaces, overblown houses that looked tired from the sheer effort of standing erect. Some had lost determination and were sagging.

This had once been the section of Lofton in which to live, the Victorian badge of success; but now, as in many Southern towns, it had passed from glory and had lost its symbol of being the ultimate achievement in life. The new houses, ranch-style moderns splashed with glass, were located elsewhere, on plots of ground that in the past had been used only as cow pastures, for planting corn, or for hunting rabbits. Now the measurement of success in Lofton was the length of a house, not how many stories it stretched upward, or how many intricate wood-carvings decorated its porch banisters and roof eaves.

Miss Jenny turned from the concrete sidewalk, which had been constructed decades ago as a WPA project, onto a brick path leading to a three-story, once-white wooden house whose grayish paint was now peeling as if either ravaged by time and the elements or scorched by fire. The aged brick walkway was covered with a deep green fungus so thick it made the bricks appear to have been painted. The grounds were planted heavily with wisteria, crepe myrtle, rosebud, dogwood, oak, and magnolia. Most of the yard, now bare of grass in large areas, had not seen sunlight in more than three decades.

The small woman in the long dress and wide-brimmed hat crossed the porch and opened the mahogany door with its center pane of stained glass, stepped into a dim entrance hall, then walked into an even dimmer parlor, a heavily draped room with a musty odor of never having been inhabited by anything but mice and shadows. She placed the jar gently on a coffee table in front of a plush, deeply cushioned Victorian couch, then she walked hurriedly down the hallway. She returned presently, wearing a faded red negligee and carrying a silver tray holding a decanter of sherry and two crystal wine glasses. She placed the tray on the coffee table and filled the two glasses, then she sat one glass by the Mason jar and held the other one in her right hand.

The minnow made several quick turns in the jar, creating a slight turbulence in the water, then it came to the surface, pushed its head upward and sucked air. Miss Jenny watched it silently for a moment, and then she said sweetly, "Now, now, Herman. You must relax and enjoy your sherry. Would you like a sugar cookie? I baked some this morning especially for you." The minnow darted back to the bottom of the jar and spun around and around.

In 1886 Thaddeus Lofton arrived in the indolent village of Crossroad, Mississippi. The twenty-year-old youth was leading a mule-drawn wagon loaded with pots, pans, earthenware, snake oil, pomade, tea kettles, liniment, bottled snuff and other assorted sundries. He had come south out of St. Louis, having spent his entire inheritance for his meager stock of goods.

He was not sure if his destination was Louisiana or Texas, but when he arrived in Crossroads, weary and travel-sore after weeks of wandering, Thaddeus decided to go no further. He set up shop in a tent and did a fair amount of business, especially with the illiterate black field hands and the poor-white tenant farmers. He devised a system whereby they could pay twenty-five cents per week for five years on an item that sold for $4.95, and his customers never kept track of the total amount paid or seemed to care so long as they could meet the weekly payments. For each additional item they purchased for $2 and under, he only added five cents to the customer's weekly payment. "Yes-sir, Mistuh Lofton, sir, that sure seems fair to me," they would say. In five years he prospered to the point of building a small wood-frame store, and five years later this was replaced by an ever larger store.

In 1900 a Chicago syndicate established a sawmill at Crossroads, and the town prospered. The citizens decided to get a charter, hold an election and select a mayor and a board of aldermen. The first business of the new board was to rename the town Lofton, in honor of the town's leading merchant, Thaddeus Lofton. This pleased Thaddeus tremendously, and he responded by immediately constructing the town's first brick building to house his expanding business. The new store had two plate-glass display windows on each side of the front entrance, and across the top, set in imported Italian marble, blazed the words: LOFTON MERCANTILE COMPANY—Established 1886—Thaddeus Lofton, Proprietor. On opening day of the new store there were free hot dogs and lemonade and fireworks that night.

By 1905 Thaddeus had acquired a respectable pot belly which he draped with a solid gold watch chain. He decided it was time to procure himself a wife, so he built the three-story Victorian house. After a brief courtship, he married the nineteen year-old daughter of a successful farmer in the south end of the county. Jenny was born nine months later.

Jenny grew up in a world of strict routine and stifling solemnity. Each meal was eaten at exactly the same time each day; no food, water or fuel was wasted, no clothing replaced unless absolutely necessary. The accumulation of wealth was the one overwhelming purpose of life.

At age ten Jenny was told about the horrors and evils of sex; she immediately joined the Baptist Church and was baptized. She was forbidden to take part in any sexually-integrated activity—with the exception of school and church.

It was evident from early on that she was destined to be a homely creature. "Never mind, dear," her mother would whisper to her, "you'll still marry someday," and Jenny never doubted. After all, she was the daughter of the man for whom Lofton was named, a man growing wealthier all the time. This would offset her unattractive features.

Life for her settled into myriad days, myriad years of expecting, hoping, thinking that the next day something would happen, some miracle would bring forth from the unknown something or someone to break the chains of the drab life that bound her to Lofton and to the huge Victorian house saturated with avarice and routine. But that day did not come. She even missed her high school senior prom. Thaddeus proclaimed, "Dancing is an invention of the devil," so she sat in her room alone and listened to music and laughter drift from the nearby school gym. The magnolias grew taller and blocked out the sun, the dogwood bloomed in the spring and turned stark in winter, and the house aged and needed to be repainted; but Jenny grew only in height, and the frequency of her fantasies increased.

Then the great crash of 1929 boomed through Lofton, clapping up and down the surrounding hills and hollows like a thunderstorm. The sawmill closed, and the cotton market vanished. The local bank failed, and with it went most of Thaddeus Lofton's shrewdly accumulated cash. He went home and cursed God and the government so violently that his wife dropped dead of a heart attack. She was buried with great pomp and ceremony, in the cheapest casket the local funeral home had in stock.

Jenny took over the job of cook, housekeeper and foot-servant as her father vigorously went about the business of trying to recoup some of his wealth. He fleeced everyone who came into his store, using the same methods he had employed in the beginning. But he put no money in the bank when it reopened. "Bankers are skunks," he proclaimed constantly to Jenny and to anyone else who would listen. "They can suck the insides from an egg without cracking the shell." He kept his money in a strongbox under his bed.

After two years of paranoid obsession of regaining his lost assets, his health failed. He sold the store and retired to the seclusion of the Victorian house, spending most of his time locked in his bedroom, counting and then recounting the money in the strongbox. Jenny was reduced to the status of servant. She was respected but not sought by Lofton citizens. "Poor Jenny," they would say, "what a devoted sweet girl, giving up her own life to take care of her dear old father." When he died in 1935, the town buried him with great pomp and ceremony. Jenny selected the cheapest coffin the local funeral home had in stock.

The dirt was still being shoveled on top of the casket when Jenny pulled the strongbox from under the bed. Her eyes gleamed as she counted the bills, saw the pile of stocks and bonds. Forty thousand dollars in cash. The next day she secretly caught the train to Midvale, in neighboring Stonewall County, and purchased several items of new clothing, among them a chic red negligee. She returned cheerfully to Lofton and waited for the suitors to flock to her door.

But none came. She was treated with dignity and respect, referred to now as Miss Jenny—that and nothing more. She waited patiently and expectantly for almost a year, then she decided it would be better to sell the house and leave Lofton. She would go someplace where she would not be known only as Old Man Lofton's thirty-year-old spinster daughter, associated both physically and spiritually only with the Victorian house and the Baptist Church.

She made her plans carefully, keeping them a strict secret, and was ready to consult a lawyer in Midvale about selling the house. Then Herman arrived. Herman Lutz, salesman from Chicago. He got off the train with a suitcase full of kitchen gadgets that would peel and slice a potato in less than twenty seconds. Tall, thirty, black-haired, smiling constantly—dressed in a brown Sears Roebuck suit, brown patent leather shoes, yellow tie and a fake diamond stickpin, and wearing a straw hat. On his second day in Lofton he knocked at the door of Miss Jenny Lofton, the potato peeler-slicer in his hand and a broad grin on his face.

What exactly happened during that first meeting with Herman, the precise sequence of events, Miss Jenny could not remember. She could vaguely recall his coming into the kitchen, demonstrating the potato gadget, then her making him a cup of tea, sitting in the parlor, telling him about herself and her father, about the town. All else was blank.

The next afternoon, Friday, Herman arrived at the prearranged time of two sharp, she opened the door anxiously and stood there smiling, She had removed a bottle of sherry from a kitchen shelf. Her father bought it for medicinal purposes only—snake bite, he said. He was never bitten by a snake, and the bottle sat unopened on the shelf, gathering dust. Now it sat on the coffee table in front of the Victorian couch in the heavily draped parlor, two crystal wine glasses beside it.

Miss Jenny and Herman sat on the couch and sipped the heady wine silently. They proceeded to play hide-n-seek in various rooms of the house like children and after dark they moved out into the yard, in darkened areas where the moonlight could not reach, two vague shadows flitting about the hallowed grounds surrounding the huge Victorian house of the esteemed name-bearer of the town of Lofton. It was just before dawn when Herman left and trudged his way back to the Lofton Hotel.

A week of blinding, flooding release followed for Miss Jenny, several days of hope, of frantic grasping for time lost, time gone forever, seven days of being a woman after thirty years of being a nonentity, a spoke on the wheel of routine. They would sip wine, then Herman would take her hand, gaze deeply into her eyes and say sweetly through his waxed mustache, "Ah, Jenny, my love, my beloved. You are my Garden of Eden, the moon and the stars, the purpose of my life. Without you I was empty, a shell, nothing, a mind without thought. Now I am a man with a grasp on life."

Jenny would say, "Oh, Herman, my love, why has it come so late?" They spoke of marriage, of their future life together in the Victorian house on the most fashionable street in the town named after her father.

They had parted that day with more talk of marriage, but the next day he did not return. She was not alarmed, for he would return. But Herman did not return that day, or the next, or the next, or ever. It was a week before she discovered that the money was also gone, vanished along with Herman. He left the stocks and bonds, but took the cash. Herman had robbed her not only of the major portion of her assets, but he had also taken her passport, her only key to the cage. The iron jaws of Lofton snapped shut on Miss Jenny.

She took all the cash that had not been in the strongbox, secretly caught the train to Jackson and engaged a private detective firm to hunt down Herman and her money; but she cautioned them to be discreet, to never let anyone in Lofton know she was even acquainted with a Herman Lutz. They never found him. There was no trace of a Herman Lutz in Chicago or in Memphis or St. Louis or anywhere. It was as if he never existed. The cage was locked tight.

Dividends from the stocks and bonds would not be enough to support Miss Jenny and pay taxes, so she did the only thing a spinster of genteel birth and supposed financial means could do with dignity—she took a job in the Lofton Public Library. The town smiled and said, "Ah, Miss Jenny is bored. She has taken a job to find some purpose in life. This is a good and noble thing for her to do."

Her life fell into a harsh routine. She had to be frugal and manage carefully lest someone discover her true financial dilemma and the cause of it, especially the cause. The shame and humiliation would be as bad or worse than the loss of the money.

On Mondays she purchased a pound of calf's liver, which she portioned into three meals. Wednesdays she purchased a chicken. The two legs were for Wednesday supper and Thursday lunch, the thighs for Thursday supper and Friday lunch. The back and neck went into soup, and the breast was reserved for a Sunday feast. On Saturdays she would have a patty of ground beef. Twice a week it was waffles for breakfast, and at other times, it was hot tea and a bun. Vegetables came from a small garden she planted in the back yard.

The activities of her life also fell into a harsh routine. She became the town's pillar of religion. On Sunday mornings she attended Sunday School and worship services at the Baptist Church, and that night, evening services. She always sat in the same pew, the pew knowingly reserved for Miss Jenny. Monday night was devoted to Missionary Circle; Wednesday night, Prayer Meeting. And to escape the indomitable walls of the stifling Victorian house, she filled in other nights by joining anything available that would give her a few hours of release—the Women's Literary Study Club, the Garden Club, and the Audubon Society. She even attended meetings of the Parents and Teachers Association. The town sighed and said, "Ah, that

Miss Jenny, what a paragon of civic virtue, attending P.T.A. meetings although she has no children. She has the welfare of Lofton in her heart."

For a few years she was deluged with sugar cookies and homemade candy, which were a godsend to her. They were brought to her by children whose parents forced them to take something to the old spinster who had all that Lofton loot and no one to leave it to. She would answer the knock, and they would be standing on the porch, scrubbed clean and neatly dressed. They would force a smile, hold forth their gift and say rapidly, "I brought you something, Miss Jenny. I love you." Then they would turn and scamper like rabbits back across the fungus-coated bricks, as if fleeing from an apparition. And after some years even this stopped. In time she was referred to by the younger generation of Lofton not as "That sweet Miss Jenny" but as "That weird old bitch who lives in the run-down house."

And Miss Jenny read books by the hundreds, starting on one shelf in the library and working her way to another. She took them home with her, and many times at daybreak she would be sitting by the lamp, still turning pages. She became an authority not only in the field of fiction, but also on archeology, mechanical engineering, the architecture of Europe, and Greek mythology.

On rare occasions she was invited to social functions, and she once attended a wedding reception. She stood there among the gaily dressed people, wearing her frayed blue dress and floppy white hat. On a table covered with lace sat an array of silver and fine crystal. The center of the table was occupied by a Fostoria bowl of champagne punch. When she started toward the punch bowl, a woman who was Miss Jenny's age but looked ten years younger grabbed her by the arm and said protectively, "Let me get you a cup of hot tea, Miss Jenny." Then she stood there alone and isolated, alone in the room, alone in the crowd, alone in the world, with a cup of hot tea in her hand as she gazed longingly at the bowl of iced champagne. Thus it went always, as if life itself was saying to her, "Ah, Miss Jenny, the trivial little sins of the flesh are not for you. You are too good, too fine, too noble to succumb to frailties."

Miss Jenny's life changed the night she took home a book on tropical fish. The idea did not strike her immediately—it seeped in gradually, like blood oozing from a small cut. When it did crystallize, she became obsessed. She ordered an aquarium from the Sears Roebuck catalog, and then she made a special trip to Jackson for the other things she needed. When everything was assembled, she asked her supervisor at the library for every Friday afternoon off. The request was readily granted. After all, Miss Jenny deserved an afternoon of rest each week. She was the library's most devoted employee, and she was a titan in the areas of civic and spiritual leadership. Nothing was too good for Miss Jenny—at least, being off on Friday afternoon wasn't.

Miss Jenny placed two empty wine glasses on the coffee table. She looked at the Mason jar and said tenderly, "It's time now, Herman, my love, my life. Our time has come again." The minnow thrashed about in the confining jar.

She grasped the jar and carried it gently up the stairs and into her father's bedroom. The aquarium sat on a metal stand beside the somber, musty-smelling bed. For a moment she held the jar tenderly. She sighed, "Oh, Herman," and then she dumped the jar's contents into the inescapable, imponderable trap with its eternal bubbles drifting upward from the neverceasing air pump.

Her tired flesh seemed to become taut again. She smiled rapturously and trembled. The smile gradually changed to a grotesque grin. She giggled, then she laughed hideously as the piranhas attacked the terrified minnow, ripping it viciously, devouring it instantly in one brief frozen moment of time in a dilapidated Victorian house on a somnolent street in the small town of Lofton.

Clem Bailey spat across the sidewalk, looked up and said, "Here she comes, boys. She's gonna make it 'bout ten seconds till two. Looks like you'll win today, Grover."

"How much is in the pot?"

"Forty-five cents."

They all tipped their hats and said, "Afternoon, Miss Jenny," as she passed in review.

Joe Clayton said, "Afternoon, Miss Jenny. Something I can do for you?"

"I would like one minnow, if you please."

The men watched silently as she left the store and walked rapidly along the sidewalk, gingerly holding the Mason jar containing the frightened, trapped minnow—the long dress swirling, the wide-brimmed hat flapping.

One then said, "I wonder what she does with it."

"Don't know. It sure beats the hell out of me."

Joe Clayton said, "Ole Miss Jenny might be kinda queer for minnows, fellows, but she's a mighty fine woman. Yessir, a mighty fine woman. If ever the Lord had a faithful servant, it's her."

"You can say that again," Clem Bailey responded as he spat a brown stream into the gutter. "It's the gospel truth. She ain't got a sin marked against her, and there ain't none left like Miss Jenny."

"Well, the Lord will take her for sure someday," Marv Sutter said, "but I'd still like to know what she does with them damned minnows."

The Demise of Bester Boo Boo

THE DEMISE OF BESTER BOO BOO

At first they named me Sylvester. Then it was shortened to Bester, and somehow, as a joke, they got to calling me Bester Boo Boo. But I didn't mind. They were good humans and I didn't care if they called me Alice, as long as I got my way—which I did.

But you know how us tomcats are. I had it made, then blew the whole deal. Curiosity. Man, do us tomcats have curiosity. If there's a hole available, we've just got to stick our heads into it. And if there's a pipe half our size, we've just got to squeeze through it somehow. Curiosity. That's what finally did it to me.

You should have seen me when they first got me. I'd never had a square meal in my life. In fact, all I'd ever eaten was crickets and rats, and I wadn't too good at catching them. I was nothing but bones and fur. But right away I knew I'd come to the right place. I turned up my big eyes, let out a mellow sad meow, and they almost had a fight over who would feed me first. Catfood, meat, fish, bowls of milk—the whole works. Was I ever happy. And I had four laps to choose from. They snatched me around among themselves like as if I was the only tomcat left.

They had a dog, but it didn't take us too long to get things settled. One of those funny short kind with a screw tail and a face that looked like it had been pushed in—they called him Pug. Well, ole Pug let me know right away who was boss in that house, but I didn't mind that either. I knew we could get along, and if one of the humans wanted a dog in their lap they'd grab Pug, and if they wanted a cat they'd grab me. There was plenty of laps to go around. And don't all humans want a dog and a cat at the same time. I mean, in their lap—cause in a situation like that, most anything could happen. So ole Pug and me came to an understanding. He'd have first shot at laps, and he'd layoff the catfood if I wouldn't bother the bones and candy. Suited me. Tomcats don't eat candy noways. And I could snitch a bone before he missed it. Dog's ain't got much sense, you know. Leastwise, not like us tomcats has.

You see, I wadn't much to look at at first. One of them gray alleycat types. None of that fancy blood in me. No, sir, I was a straight-line alleycat, right off the trash dump. And that's good. Makes a cat appreciate things more when he gets them, gets took up with some good humans. Especially if you ain't had nothing to eat but crickets and rats. But the moment I walked into that house I knew Christmas had come for me. Boiled shrimp! You got any idea how boiled shrimp tastes to a cat? You don't? Well, fellow, if you think watermelon and grapes is good, you just don't know nothing. Boiled shrimp.

Sometimes they'd put me out at night. But I didn't mind that either. Tomcats has lots of business transactions to make at night. I mean—well, you know. Female cats. Anyhow, at first they put a box of sand in the kitchen. Sometimes it seems that humans can be about as dumb as dogs. I got the idea. But you think a tomcat like me was going to do something foolish and blow the whole bit? Not a chance, Buster. They didn't need no sand box. I got better sense than that. Besides, us alley cat types has got a certain amount of self-respect. I ain't that stupid. Raw oysters! Fellow, you ain't got no idea.

And late ever afternoon all four of um, the two big uns and the two little uns, would take ole Pug walking. I sat there behind a bush and watched it the first time. Then the second time I just decided I'd go too. A dog ain't the only one that enjoys walking with humans. So here I'd trot along with them, my tail standing straight up like a flagpole, and them humans nigh-on had a fit. They ain't never seen no tomcat before that liked to go walking. Ole Pug didn't fancy the idea too much. He figured I was cutting in on him some. So he'd tear off in four directions, barking like an idiot at nothing, but I'd just keep right on trottin. Didn't make me no difference. But them humans'd just laugh and say, Look at that crazy tomcat go. And fried fish! They'd even cook an egg just for me for breakfast.

Wadn't long before I'd just about doubled. I looked plumb like a butterball. It made some of the other cats around the neighborhood jealous. Didn't bother me none. All I'd have to do was look up and meow, and they'd be bowls all over the floor. I got to where I ate about fifteen times a day, what time I wadn't sleeping. Sometimes I'd meow when I wadn't even hungry, just to watch um jump. And then sometimes they'd go away and leave me alone for two-three days. I'd make out all right, cause you know how us alleycats are. Crickets and rats. But when they'd come back I'd stagger around like I was about to faint, and I'd meow real low, like as if I was so weak I could hardly stand up. They'd snatch me up, run in the house and dump the whole refrigerator on the floor. You ever tasted pure cream? Fellow, us tomcats ain't dumb.

And they had these great big ole glass doors at the back of the house, in the room where the table was, next to the kitchen. Ever morning I'd know just about what time one of the big uns would pass through that room on the way to the kitchen, so I'd be sitting there waiting, just sitting outside that glass door, looking pitiful. She'd slide that glass door open and in I'd trot. One meow and it was bacon and eggs. Sometimes I'd fool her though, like tomcats is prone to do. They was a window right over the kitchen sink. I'd jump up there and lay down. Then she'd come in looking, and I wouldn't be by the glass door, and she'd get all excited. After awhile she'd come on in the kitchen, and there I'd be, plopped on that ledge, staring at her through the window. Fellow, you ever eat any of that canned catfood made out of ground-up fish?

Curiosity. That's what did it to me. I'd been in lots of scrapes before. Hung up in pipes. Trapped under the house. Caught in trees. One time I even crawled up inside the heatpump, and they had to take the top off to get me out. But that night I jumped down in a dark hole and I just couldn't get out. I tried, cause I was thinking about that bowl of milk they always sat outside the door when they put me out at night. In case I got hungry before morning. But I just couldn't make it, no matter what I'd do. Don't know how long I stayed in that hole, but it was a heap of time. I got plumb skinny before it was over. Then I got real tired, and sleepy, and I lay down. When I woke up, I just floated right up out of that hole. Just floated out. Only my body stayed behind. Curiosity.

I was trotting home just like always, only there wadn't really no me. So when I got to the glass door, they was all standing there looking out, sort of crying, and I was looking in, and I was seeing them, only they wadn't seeing me, cause they wadn't really no me to see. And I'd meow real loud, but they couldn't hear it no more. I still hang around, though, and they put that bowl of milk out ever night. Some dumb dog comes along and laps it up, but they still put it out. And I still trot along when they take ole Pug walking, my tail standing straight up like a flagpole. Ever little piece they'll stop and look around, like as if they expect me to pop right out of a bush. And ever time one of them humans pass that glass door they stop and look, real sad like. I bet they do it forty times a day.

Curiosity. That's the way it goes with us tomcats.

A Pair of Blue Shoes

A PAIR OF BLUE SHOES

Cathy Flanagan stood in front of a display window of Banks Mercantile Store, staring at a pair of shoes. They were blue with silver buckles and white straps. She had been there for a half-hour, peering through the fly-specked glass, her eyes transfixed on what seemed to her to be the most beautiful pair of shoes ever created. She finally turned and went into the store reluctantly.

Clifton Banks came from behind a counter and said, "Why, hello, Cathy. Haven't seen you in some time. How's your ma and pa?"

"They're fine." She clasped her hands together and cast her eyes downward.

"Something I can do for you?" Banks asked, noticing her uncertainty.

"How much are they?" Cathy asked.

"How much is what, Cathy?"

"The shoes. The blue shoes in the window."

"Oh," Banks said. "The blue shoes. Let me show them to you." He removed the shoes from the display window and handed them to her.

Cathy took them hesitantly, holding them as if grasping something that would shatter if dropped. She put them against her face and inhaled deeply, smelling the fragrance of new leather. Then she said again, "How much?"

Banks scratched his head as he looked into her anxious eyes. He said, "Well, Cathy, they're real fine shoes, the best I have in the store, but it seems that everybody wants black or brown shoes, not blue. You can have them for five dollars. You want to try them on?"

"No," she said quickly. "No. I better not. Thank you, Mister Banks." Then she turned and hurried from the store.

He walked to the front door and watched her run down the sidewalk, her oversize brogans making a clomping sound as she rushed toward the vacant lot where the country folks parked their wagons. Then he looked down at the shoes still in his hands. He wished he had just given them to her, then he shook his head and went back to the counter.

Cathy sat down beside a clump of wisteria at the edge of the lot and watched as people walked along the sidewalk. Several town girls, dressed in fresh cotton dresses and black leather shoes, laughed and giggled as they passed by. Then she looked down at the brogan shoes, passed down to her by another tenant family, and at her white dress, made by her mother from flour sacks. She suddenly ran to the wagon and climbed in, wishing that her mother and father would hurry back so they could leave.

Cathy sat on the front steps of the tenant shack, watching the dying June sun bathe the red clay Mississippi soil with a glowing orange-hazel tint. She looked across the cotton fields toward the big white house of the Rodney family, the farm owners, wondering what Sallie Rodney was doing, what Sallie would have for supper.

Then she studied the green cotton plants that were springing upward from the blood-colored fields, looking intensely at the rows that seemed to stretch away into infinity. She looked up when she heard someone coming down the road. It was Clara Mae, a black girl the same age as Cathy, fourteen, who lived in a tenant shack a half-mile down the road. Her father also worked for the Rodneys.

Clara Mae turned into the yard when she saw Cathy sitting on the steps. She grinned and said, "We gone have poke fo supper. Mistuh Rodney gave Pa a chunk of smoked meat. You want me to save you a piece?"

"Guess not," Cathy said. "Ma'll fix us something."

Clara Mae studied Cathy's face closely, then she said, "You worried 'bout something? You ain't been sick, has you?"

"I need to earn five dollars," Cathy said solemnly.

"Five dollars?" Clara Mae questioned, looking at Cathy with puzzlement. "How come? Whut fo you needs all that?"

"To buy some shoes in Midvale."

"How come?" Clara Mae asked, still baffled. "Something wrong with yo brogans?"

"Not really," Cathy sighed. "But these shoes are blue."

"I ain't never had no blue shoes neither," Clara Mae said. "I kin help you some. Miz Rodney gives me fifty cents to do her wash ever Satterdy. You help me, you kin have half."

"That wouldn't be fair," Cathy frowned. "You'd be losing half your pay."

~79~

"Don't make me no never mind. I jus gives it to Ma anyway. I don't need no blue shoes."

"Can I start this week?" Cathy asked anxiously.

"Sho. An Mistuh Rodney's payin ten cents a hour to extra hands fer choppin. Maybe you can do some of that too."

"Maybe," Cathy said. "I have to help Ma most of the time, cause she's been ailin lately. But maybe I can chop some."

Clara Mae turned to leave, then she hesitated a moment and said, "You goin to church with me Sunday?"

"Yes, I'll go," Cathy replied. She always attended the black church since there was no white church nearby, and it was too far to go in the wagon to attend services in Midvale. And even if she could go with someone into Midvale, she did not want to enter the church wearing brogan shoes and a flour sack dress.

Clara called back, "I'll come by fer you Satterdy moanin at eight."

"Thanks, Clara Mae," Cathy said. "I'll be ready."

Cathy sat at the bare plank table bathed by the soft sulphurish light of a coal oil lamp. Her mother sat across from her, patching a rip in a blue denim work shirt. Her father was in a corner of the room, rocking gently, his huge calloused hands resting on his knees.

Cathy scribbled on a piece of brown wrapping paper, calculating that if she chopped cotton for two hours each day she could earn a dollar in a week, and with the twenty-five cents each Saturday for helping with the wash her earnings would amount to a dollar twenty-five. She frowned, then she smiled when she realized that in four weeks she could have the necessary amount of money.

She looked up into her mother's face and said hopefully, "Ma, will it be all right if I chop for two hours a day and help Clara Mae with Miz Rodney's wash on Saturday morning? It won't bother with getting my chores done."

The woman's hands stopped the needle halfway through the faded cloth. "How come you want to do that?" she asked. "Choppins mighty hard in this heat."

"There's some blue shoes at Banks Mercantile Store I want to buy. I can earn the money in a month."

Cathy's mother looked at her with a pained expression, then she said simply, "I guess."

Her father shifted his gaze to the young face, the flowing blonde hair and deep-set blue eyes. He knew she deserved better than this drab dismal room of a tenant shack surrounded by a barren yard where chickens had long ago pecked away the last remaining blade of grass, leaving only blood-colored clay. He wished he could take her into town and buy the shoes for her, but he knew this was impossible. He got up quickly and left the room.

Cathy and Clara Mae stood by the huge black-iron wash pot, watching the milky water as it bubbled and sent up a grayish swirling smoke vapor. The pine knots beneath the pot sizzled and popped, sending orange sparks cascading across the ground.

Clara Mae said, "You jog an I'll hang. That water's too hot fer you, an you not used to it. Them clothes would burn yo hands jus by touchin um."

Cathy took a broom handle and jogged the clothes up and down in the boiling water, then she fished out several pieces on the end of the stick and let them drop into a large pan. Clara then took the steaming garments and walked across the yard toward the clothes line, where she would hang them up.

Cathy continued the jogging as Sallie Rodney walked up and watched. Sallie, the same age as Cathy, wore a cotton print dress and black leather shoes. She said, "How come you're doing that?"

"I need to earn some money," Cathy replied, continuing to agitate the garments. "Clara Mae said I could help her. I didn't ask her. She just said I could."

"That's trash work," Sallie said distastefully. How come you're doing trash work?"

"Taint neither," Cathy said quickly. "My ma does her wash ever week."

"That's different. That's your own wash. This is our wash. It's trash work."

Cathy turned away from Sallie and looked down into the boiling murky water in the huge black-iron pot, watching the fine garments as they rose to the top and hung suspended for a moment; then they disappeared beneath the surface and were replaced immediately by other garments repeating the cycle—endless motion caused by the popping fire and tumultuous water. Without looking up, she said to Sallie, "Don't make no never mind. Clara Mae said I could help her."

Sallie turned and started back toward the house. She looked back and said, "It's still trash work."

Clara Mae returned with the empty pan. She looked at Cathy, seeing the pained expression in Cathy's eyes, then she said, "What'd she say to you?"

"Nothing. Not much, anyway."

"You still want to help?" Clara Mae asked, knowing inborn what Sallie had probably said to her.

"Yes," Cathy said firmly. "I'll jog and you hang."

Cathy stopped for a moment, adjusted the sunbonnet and wiped sweat from her forehead; then she leaned against the hoe and watched other workers striking at the ground around cotton plants. Far in the distance, in an adjoining quarter of land, she could see her father following a plow, his black felt hat pulled down to his eyebrows, his hunched back straining against the plow line. It seemed that smoke was rising up out of the land, that each stroke of a hoe, and each gash cut by a plow, created a vent for the release of a smoldering fire somewhere beneath the red surface.

Cathy gripped the hoe and continued striking. She shifted her mind away from the cotton field and into the realm of imagination, remembering things seen and not seen, trying to think of anything but the length of the row and the blistering sun.

Mr. Banks had once given her a calendar which she still kept under her bed. Each season was illustrated with a picture, and the spring picture was of a white cottage surrounded by roses and sunflower and pansies and a rainbow of other flowers.

Summer was a scene of girls in lace-bordered white dresses, spreading a picnic lunch beneath a huge oak tree beside a placid lake, the boys standing by a surrey, watching. Fall was a golden sea of leaves, with snow capped mountains in the background.

And winter—the December scene blotted out the heat and the sweat; she could see people gathered around a Christmas tree, opening packages, new shoes and sweaters and dresses, hair ribbons, bottles of perfume, all gleaming and all new.

Clara Mae shook Cathy's shoulder and said anxiously, "Is you all right?"

"Yes," Cathy answered, startled. "I'm fine."

"If you feel bad you best quit. Too much sun makes you sick. You look like you had too much sun."

"I'm fine," Cathy said again, striking vigorously at the soil around a cotton plant.

Cathy sat at the table counting the coins, the soft glow of the coal oil lamp accentuating the brownness of her face. She was not thinking of the long hours spent by the boiling wash pot or the sweltering heat of the fields—she was seeing the blue shoes. She smiled when she wrapped the coins in a piece of cloth and tied them into a knot.

Then her thoughts turned to Sallie Rodney, hovering in the background, staring at her distastefully, the huge white house looming in the background. She suddenly turned to her mother and said, "How come some folks own land and some don't?"

Her mother remained silent for a moment, furrows forming across her brow, then she finally said, "It's the Lord's will."

"How come," Cathy asked, not satisfied with the answer.

"The Lord don't say how come. He don't explain His will."

"Taint just that," her father said, breaking into the conversation. "It's not that simple, and it's not just the Lord's will. It depends some on where you were born and who you were born to."

"Then why was I born here?" Cathy asked, child-like.

"Because it's where your grandaddy stopped when he came over here from Ireland," her father said. "Maybe he should 'a kept going, but he didn't. When he died, all my brothers left, but I stayed behind to take care of Mamma while she was alive. We had our own farm, but I couldn't keep it up by myself, so I lost it for taxes. That's why you're here in this tenant shack. It's not just the will of the Lord, unless the tax collector is kin to the Lord."

Cathy did not really understand these unfamiliar words coming from her father. She turned back to her mother and said, "Will us and Clara Mae's folks own land someday, and have our own house?"

"Maybe someday," her mother replied. "It depends on the will of the Lord."

Cathy sat on the rear of the wagon, watching the wheels cut narrow ruts in the dirt road. She wished her father would strap the mule and hurry them along.

Clara Mae had been there when they left, grinning broadly, sharing Cathy's delight. She said, "You be sho an come let me see um soon's you git back."

"I will, Clara Mae," Cathy said assuringly. "You'll be the first to see them."

Cathy dared not think what she would do if the shoes were gone. She had thought about this beside the wash pot and in the fields, and at night when her hands and arms ached. But now she was sure they would be there; they would be, they must be.

She jumped from the wagon before her father could tie the mule, then she ran blindly along the sidewalk. Her heart stopped when she reached the display window and the shoes were not there. She rushed into the store and cried, "Are they gone Mister Banks? Are they gone?"

"What, Cathy?" Banks said, startled. "Is what gone?"

"The shoes! The blue shoes!"

Banks relaxed as he said gently, "No, Cathy, they're not gone. I changed the window. They're still here. You want to see them again?"

"Yes," she said eagerly, the color coming back into her face. "I've got the money now."

Banks went into a back room and returned with the shoes. He handed them to her and said, "You better see first if they fit."

Cathy unlaced one brogan, stepped out of it, and put her foot slowly into the gleaming blue leather. She closed her eyes as if in prayer when the shoe fit perfectly.

"You want to wear them, or do you want me to put them in a box," Banks asked.

"Put them in a box," Cathy said. "I'll wear them to church tomorrow. Here's the money." She handed him the worn cloth containing the coins.

"I'll count it later," he said. "You go on now."

Cathy walked back toward the parking lot, holding the box gently. Three boys stood idly on the sidewalk, watching her approach. Two were sixteen, the other a year older. The oldest stepped out and said, "What you got in that box, Cathy?"

"Shoes," she beamed. "You want to see?" She opened the box and held it forward.

"What's a dumb twit piece of white trash like you want with blue shoes?" the boy asked. "You going to wear them with that flour sack dress?"

Another boy said, "Sallie Rodney told us what you did to earn the money."

The oldest boy grabbed the box, jerked out the shoes and shouted, "Forward pass! Ketch it on the run!" He threw one shoe into the air and the other two boys scampered after it.

Cathy looked on in horror and disbelief, feeling a wave of nausea sweep through her. She screamed, "Stop it! Stop it!" She ran after them, chasing them down the street, screaming and seeing the blue shoes sail into the air and crash into the dust, then be picked up again and kicked into a spinning whirling ball of tumbling color.

She ran after them for two blocks, then they cut across a vacant lot and came to a clearing along the creek bank. She chased them frantically, crying and pleading, but they kept just out of reach, teasing her. One boy shouted "Forward punt," then one shoe went spinning through the air and landed in the middle of the creek. For a moment rings formed around the splash and spread outward, then they were swept away with the current.

Cathy fell to her knees and sobbed bitterly as a fat black woman charged into the boys, swinging a walking cane, striking them on the head and shoulders, shouting, "You boys stop dat! Stop right now! I's gwine tell yo folks! You leave dat chile alone!"

One of the boys dropped the remaining shoe, then they all ran back across the clearing, chanting, "Cathy is a dumb twit, Cathy is a dumb twit."

The woman looked down at Cathy and said angrily, "I's Doshie. I cooks fa Mistuh Thonton. He a lawyer. I'm gwine tell him 'bout dis. He'll fix dem boys good. Mean devils!" Then she took Cathy by the arm, lifted her up and said, "Is you all right, chile?"

Cathy wiped her eyes with her hand, smearing dirt across her face. She looked at the woman and tried to smile, then she picked up the tattered shoe. For a moment she held it gently, then she dropped it into the dust and walked silently back toward the wagon, the oversize brogans clamping profoundly against the blood-colored earth.

Fried Mullet and Grits

FRIED MULLET AND GRITS

It was mid-afternoon when Alvin Binder pulled the black Buick Regal off the two-lane asphalt highway and came to a stop on the right shoulder. Across the road, adjacent to a sandy lane leading off into the woods, there was a faded red sign:

TURKEY CREEK FISH CAMP
BOATS - BAIT - CABINS
2 MILES

On an impulse he pulled across the highway and started down the narrow lane. Huge oak trees formed an overhead canopy, and beneath them were thick clumps of palmetto surrounded by a carpet of ferns.

He drove slowly, glancing both right and left, wondering if this were the right thing to do. If he kept going he could make Fort Lauderdale by nightfall.

The lane made a right turn and then came into a clearing bordered on the south by a slow flowing stream, and then a long stretch of sawgrass. On the left there was an unpainted building with a porch on its front. Off to the right side there was a row of six small cabins, also unpainted and highly weathered.

Alvin Binder parked the car and went inside the main building. Behind a counter there were shelves filled with canned goods, and a cooler to the left contained beer, soda and milk. Just then a short rotund man came from a room at the rear of the store. He was about the same age as Alvin, sixty-five, and his face was burned leather brown. He said, "Howdy. Something I can do for you?"

For a moment Alvin didn't know if the man could do something for him or not. He finally said, "Well, I don't know. I was on my way to Fort Lauderdale and saw your sign. I usually go down the turnpike, but this time I decided to take some backroads instead. I've never done this before."

The man extended his hand and said, "I'm Sim Lowry. You want something cold to drink"? A beer or a soda?"

"Coke will do fine."

Sim popped open a can and handed it to Alvin. He then said, "Where you coming from?"

"Marion, Ohio. My wife and I have been spending two weeks each year in a time share condo in Fort Lauderdale. She died six months ago, and I'm on my way there to make arrangements to sell my share of the condo. Wouldn't be the same there without Mary."

Sim could see the sadness in the stranger's eyes. He said, "You're welcome to spend the night here if you're a mind to. All the cabins are empty. The water's so low now nobody comes out here to fish. We need a real good soaking rain. Can let you have a cabin for ten bucks. There's no TV or air conditioning, but it does have a ceiling fan. And you can eat with me and the missus tonight and in the morning. No charge. Tonight we're having cooter stew, swamp cabbage and corn pone. In the morning it'll be fried mullet and grits, with some biscuits too."

"Sounds like a good deal to me," Alvin said, still a bit uncertain about what he was doing. "Which cabin do I take?"

"The first one," Sim responded. "It's not locked. Just go on over and settle in, then come back and we'll visit for a spell. That is, if you want to."

"Thanks," Alvin said. "I'll do that. I'll be back here shortly."

When he emerged from the cabin Alvin gazed southward. In the distance to the right there was a line of giant bald cypress trees, some towering 100 feet, marking the beginning of a swamp. Limbs were dotted with egrets and white ibis. Blue herons waded slowly along the shallows of the creek, pecking at something beneath the black water. To the east, sawgrass stretched away to the horizon.

Sim was sitting in a rocker on the front porch of the store, so Alvin crossed over and took a chair beside him.

"Nice and quiet out here," Alvin said.

"That's the way we like it," Sim responded. "I got no hankering for city life."

"How long have you been here?" Alvin asked curiously.

"Owned this fish camp for forty years. Before that, me and my daddy was in the cattle business up north of here. I got tired of sitting in a saddle all day, so I came down here and built this camp. We don't have any frills out here, but it suits us fine. We make do O.K. What do you do up in Ohio?"

"I owned an appliance store, but I sold it five years ago and retired. That's when we bought the time-share condo. I guess I should have bought a camper instead, and taken Mary to a lot of different places we've never seen. Like this. But it's too late for that now."

A plump woman suddenly burst through the screen door. She was wearing a blue cotton dress and white canvas shoes. She said to Alvin, "I'm Ruthie. You men come on in inside now. Swamp cabbage is best when it's piping hot. It's time to eat."

Sim and Alvin got up and followed her inside.

After supper, Sim and Alvin were back on the porch when a dusty pickup truck pulled in and parked. A man of about forty lumbered out of the truck and joined them. He was as slim as a fence rail and dressed in faded overalls without shirt or shoes. He said, "Evening, Sim. Thought I'd stop by for a beer."

"As usual," Sim said. "I'll get it for you."

Sim went into the store, returned and handed the can to the new arrival. He said, "This is Alvin Binder from Ohio. He's staying the night with us. And this varmint here who looks like a scarecrow is Junior Rawson. He lives not far from here, out in the swamp."

"Pleased to meet you," Alvin said.

"Likewise."

Junior took a deep draw on the beer and then said, "If this place is givin you the willies, it's a pity ole Biff Sutter ain't around right now. You'd get some free entertainment. Biff is always playing jokes on somebody. He was at a flea market one time and this guy had a gorilla suit for sale. It was pretty wore out, but was O.K. Biff bought it for twenty dollars.

"They's always been a rumor out here about a swamp ape. Some folks calls it a skunk ape, cause it's supposed to smell like a skunk. Some folks even swear they've seen it. Well, ole Biff got to putting on that monkey suit and running around in the woods when tourists came by in a fishing boat. He'd jump up and down and shout, 'Woogla woogla wah wah.' Scared the living daylights outen them tourists, and their eyeballs popped right out of the sockets.

"One thing he didn't figure on was Uncle Benro. He's about eighty years old, half blind, and can't hear too good either. Everywhere he goes he carries a double-barrel 12-gauge shotgun loaded with number eight birdshot, and he's liable to shoot at anything that moves. We see him coming we just hide behind a tree till he's passed by.

"One day Biff was on the bank of a canal, jumping up and down and shouting 'woogla woogla wah wah.' He didn't see Uncle Benro coming up behind him. Uncle Benro throwed up that blunderbus and unloaded both barrels right in the direction of Biff's behind. Black fur flew everywhere. That 'woogla woogla wah wah' changed to 'yipe yipe yipe,' and the last them tourists seen of Biff he was cutting through the swamp eighty miles per hour. Shortly after that, Biff traded what was left of the gorilla suit for the mangiest dog I ever seen. That dog wasn't worth a cuss for nothing, but Biff said he was going to train him to climb trees and bark like a squirrel. That would get the attention of them tourists for sure. Biggest squirrel they ever seen sitting on the limb of a tree."

Sim didn't even crack a smile, but Alvin erupted in laughter. Alvin finally said, "Seems you have some characters out here."

"That ain't nothing," Junior said. "You stay around for awhile I'll tell you some tales that'll make your ears stand up like a rabbits."

Junior then got up, stretched, and said, "I got to go now and gig some frogs if I can scare the gators away from them. With this low water, the gators and frogs are kinda crowded together. It was good to meet you, Mister Binder. You come back and visit with us sometime."

"I just might do that," Alvin said. He watched the old pickup truck disappear around the bend of the road, then he said to Sim, "Guess I'll turn in now. It's been a long day."

"I'll roust you out for breakfast," Sim said. "You'll like fried mullet and grits. Real cracker food."

Alvin sat on the bed for a moment, then he got up and walked down to the dock. The moon was high now, casting a soft silver glow through the trees and across the sawgrass. At first he could not understand what it was that so enthralled him, and then he realized it was the absence of human sights and sounds: no street lights, no rumbling automobiles, no shrill laughter drifting upward from a crowded beach, no sirens shrieking in the night. And no television blaring in a thick-carpeted room. All he and Mary ever did in the condo at night was watch TV. They could have as well been in a New York City hotel room as a Florida condo. This thought had not occurred to him before.

The moonlight was bright enough for him to see a small stream meandering snake-like through the sawgrass, and he wondered where it led to. In the distance there was the dim outline of a shell mound—one probably built by Indians centuries ago. In his imagination he joined them, snatching roasted oysters from a roaring fire. And then he felt a sudden release, as if nature flushed all the sorrow and sadness from his mind. He wished he had brought Mary to this place, for he was sure she would have enjoyed it.

He lingered for an hour more, drinking deeply of the magic that seemed to envelop all the world; then he went back into the cabin and closed the door. He slept soundly for the first time in six months.

Breakfast was all that Sim promised., He enjoyed three helpings of fried mullet fillets and grits, four buttermilk biscuits, and six cups of strong black coffee made in an old-fashioned stove-top percolator. He felt a warm glow as he walked back to the cabin and packed to leave.

Once again he gazed out at the great expanse of natural, un-touched land, wishing he had time to explore it. Next time he would.

Sim came off the porch and down to the car. He shook Alvin's hand warmly and said, "It was good to have you here, Alvin. It's a pity you don't have more time to spend with us."

"Do you reserve these cabins?" Alvin asked.

"Well, sort of," Sim said. "Some regular customers come at the same time each year, and we hold a cabin open for them. "

"I want one for the first two weeks in October each year. Can you do that?"

"I'll mark it in my book."

Alvin got into the Buick reluctantly, then he waved his hand and pointed the car back toward the asphalt highway.

Talk to the Wind

The following poem was written by sixteen-year-old Patrick Smith, in memory of a beloved elderly neighbor who loved all things in nature and was famous locally for her beautiful flower gardens.

TALK TO THE WIND

As the sands of the desert
Drift to and fro
They grind out all traces of time,
They blast and destroy the
Things of old,
And leave only dust and grime.

But there's some things that
Withstand the test
Of even the sands of time,
And the drifts of the years
And change of the tides
Can't remove what they leave behind.

They live on in name and tradition,
They always stay the same,
They live through their deeds
And their kindness,
Their love, their pride, and
Their fame.

Dwelling in the things they
Once loved,
The trees, the flowers, the wind,
They trod the paths they
Once did,
And play on your memory again.

You miss their kind voice
Greeting you,
You miss the touch of their hand,
But they're not gone
And forgotten,
Just living in another land.

So if you miss their presence,
Just stop and talk to
The wind,
And the flowers and birds
And leaves on the trees
Will talk back to you again.

~About the Author~

Patrick D. Smith is a 1999 inductee into the Florida Artists Hall of Fame, the highest and most prestigious cultural honor that can be bestowed upon an individual by the State of Florida.

In May 2002 Smith was the recipient of the Florida Historical Society's Fay Schweim Award as the "Greatest Living Floridian." The one-time-only award was established to honor the one individual who has contributed the most to Florida in recent history. Smith was cited for the impact his novels have made on Floridians, both natives and newcomers to the state, and for the worldwide acclaim he has received.

Smith has been nominated three times for the Pulitzer Prize, in 1973 for *Forever Island,* which was a 1974 selection of the Reader's Digest Condensed Book Club and has been published in 46 countries; in 1978 for *Angel City,* which was produced as a "Movie of the Week" for the CBS television network and has aired worldwide; and in 1984 for *A Land Remembered,* which was an Editors' Choice selection of the New York Times Book Review. Smith's lifetime work was nominated for the 1985 Nobel Prize for Literature, and since then he has received five additional nominations.

In 1995 Patrick Smith was elected by The Southern Academy of Letters, Arts and Science for its highest literary award, The Order of the South. Previous recipients include Eudora Welty, James Dickey, and Reynolds Price. In 1996 he was named a Florida Ambassador of the Arts, an honor given each year by the state of Florida to someone who has made significant contributions to Florida's cultural growth. In 1999 Smith was inducted into the Florida Artists Hall of Fame, which is the highest and most prestigious cultural honor the state bestows upon an individual artist. Prior inductees include writers Marjorie Kinnan Rawlings, Zora Neale Hurston, and Ernest Hemingway.

In October 1990 he received the University of Mississippi's Distinguished Alumni Award and was inducted into the University's Alumni Hall of Fame. In 1997, the Florida Historical Society created a new annual award, the Patrick D. Smith Florida Literature Award, in his honor.

To learn more about the author
and his books, visit
http://www.PatrickSmithOnline.com
the official Patrick D. Smith website.

Here you can order all of his books
and the award-winning DVD,
"Patrick Smith's Florida, A Sense of Place."